I dedicate this book to all teachers who patiently help students learn from their mistakes daily.

How Did You Miss That?

A Story for Teaching Self-Monitoring

Written by
Bryan Smith

Illustrated by
Lisa M. Griffin

BOYS TOWN
Press

Boys Town, Nebraska

D1242604

How Did You Miss That?
Text and Illustrations Copyright © 2019 by Father Flanagan's Boys' Home
ISBN: 978-1-944882-45-7

Published by the Boys Town Press
13603 Flanagan Blvd.
Boys Town, NE 68010

For a Boys Town Press catalog, call **1-800-282-6657**
or visit our website: **BoysTownPress.org**

Publisher's Cataloging-in-Publication Data

Names: Smith, Bryan (Bryan Kyle), 1978- author. | Griffin, Lisa M., 1972- illustrator.

Title: How did you miss that? : a story for teaching self-monitoring / written by Bryan Smith ; illustrated by Lisa M. Griffin.

Description: Boys Town, NE : Boys Town Press, [2019] | Series: Executive FUNction. | Audience: grades K-6. | Summary: The latest installment in the Executive FUNction series follows Braden as he learns the importance of self-monitoring and some good strategies to help him slow down, recognize (and prevent!) mistakes, and stay on track.--Publisher.

Identifiers: ISBN: 978-1-944882-45-7

Subjects: LCSH: Self-monitoring--Juvenile fiction. | Self-management (Psychology) for children-- Juvenile fiction. | Errors--Prevention--Juvenile fiction. | Children--Time management-- Juvenile fiction. | Stress management for children--Juvenile fiction. | Self-reliance in children--Juvenile fiction. | Children--Life skills guides--Juvenile fiction. | CYAC: Errors--Prevention--Fiction. | Time management--Fiction. | Stress management--Fiction. | Self-reliance--Fiction. | Conduct of life--Fiction. | BISAC: JUVENILE FICTION / Social Themes / Self-Esteem & Self-Reliance. | JUVENILE FICTION / Social Themes / Values & Virtues. | SELF-HELP / Self-Management / Time Management. | JUVENILE NON-FICTION / Social Topics / Self-Esteem & Self Reliance. | EDUCATION / Counseling / General.

Classification: LCC: PZ7.1.S597 H68 2019 | DDC: [Fic]--dc23

Printed in the United States
10 9 8 7 6 5 4 3 2 1

Boys Town Press is the publishing division of Boys Town, a national organization serving children and families.

Hey everyone.

It's me, Braden.

Do your parents act like you have nothing better to do **than chores?**

Mine sure do. They're always telling me to clean this and clean that.

It happened just the other night. I got home from a late baseball game, and my parents told me to quickly get ready for bed. Just as I do every night, I checked my nightly list.

Braden's List

1. Brush teeth

2. Take a shower

3. Clean
   everything up

Three things.
Not too hard,
as you can see.

Blake's List

1. Put homework
   in folder

2. Lay out clothes

3. Brush teeth

5

That night, I was pretty sure I set a new world record. I did all three things in 4 minutes and 33 seconds! I couldn't wait to see Mom's face when she saw how fast I got everything done.

But when she walked in my room, **I could tell something was Wrong.**

"Braden, didn't I tell you to get ready for bed?" Mom asked.

"You sure did," I said. "I thought you would be proud of me. I checked my list and **did it all in 4:33 flat!"**

"Not so fast. Come with me," Mom said. We walked to my bathroom.

"Now Braden, I see you did the first two items on your nightly checklist and I am proud of you for that.

Did you forget about the third one, clean everything up?"

8

I explained, **"No, of course not! I rinsed the sink!"**

"Right, but how did you miss that?" Mom said, pointing to the messy mirror, the puddles of water, and the blob of toothpaste. *"It looks like something* **EXPLODED** in here!"

9

Mom told me I needed to do a better job of "self-monitoring" when I was trying to accomplish something.

"Braden, there are

4 STEPS to self-Monitoring.

#1 Think about what you are trying to accomplish.

#2 Stay focused on that goal until the end.

#3 When finished, check your work again, and make sure EVERYTHING is done.

#4 Ask for help if you get stuck."

12

I quickly cleaned up all the things Mom had pointed out.

"Now Braden, before you leave the bathroom, I want you to check your list one more time and make sure **EVERYTHING** is done. I see you hung your towel up, which is great. Do you see anything else that needs to be put away?"

As I was looking around trying to figure it out, I felt something under my feet.

"Oh yeah, my dirty clothes!" I quickly put
my shirt and pants in the hamper.

"I knew your self-monitoring skills were in there somewhere," Mom said.

I was hoping to never hear about self-monitoring again. But sure enough, it happened at school two days later.

We were going over our math test from the day before.

I was sure I got a **100** because I knew everything on the test. As Mrs. Green put my paper on my desk, I immediately saw **"-10" written at the top.**

16

"I'm sure you did," she replied. *"Unfortunately, you didn't make sure EVERYTHING was done."*

"What do you mean?" I asked.

Mrs. Green turned to page 4 and said those words I'd heard before: "How did you **miss that?"**

As I stared at the blank page, I asked, **"How's that possible?"**

"Probably because you weren't monitoring your work," Mrs. Green said. "Your mom told me about your plan. Let's look at those steps again."

4 STEPS to Self-Monitoring

#1 Think about what you are trying to accomplish.

#2 Stay focused on that goal until the end.

#3 When finished, check your work again, and make sure EVERYTHING is done.

#4 Ask for help if you get stuck.

This time I didn't need an adult to tell me what I did wrong. **"I know, I know. I wasn't focused until the end,"** I said.

"*Right. And it doesn't look like you checked your work to make sure **EVERYTHING** was done when you finished,*" Mrs. Green added.

The good news is that Mrs. Green let me **try again for those 10 points.** The bad news is I had to miss 10 minutes of recess that day finishing my test.

I realized not monitoring my work was now interfering with my favorite part of the day – recess. I couldn't let that happen again.

That Friday at school was going to be an exciting one. My class would be book buddies with the class of my younger brother, Blake. I really like helping Blake become a better reader.

Just the other night, I was helping Blake
read this book about Sam the cat.
Blake was doing great and then said
the funniest thing.

On one of the pages, the words say:

*Mom reminded Sam to put his books in
his backpack to get ready for school.*

24

Blake said,
"Mom reminded Sam to put his **BOOTY** *in his backpack to get ready for school."*

I LAUGHED so hard I started crying.

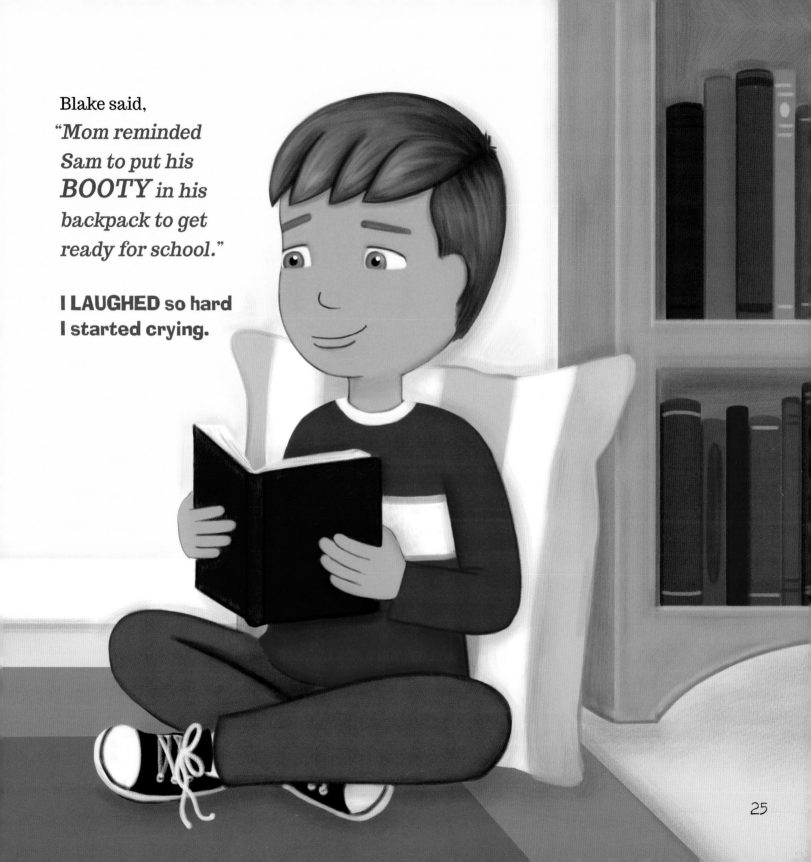

Blake looked surprised, so I said,
**"Dude, that doesn't even make sense!
How did you miss that?"**

26

I told Blake how he said **"booty"** instead of **"books."**

Then we both started laughing.

"Let me try that again," Blake said. This time he read it correctly because he was monitoring his reading.

Over the weekend, I learned adults have to monitor their work, too. Mom and Dad decided to paint the family room. Blake and I ran outside to play to "stay out of the way" (in other words, so we wouldn't have to help).

Around lunchtime, Mom and Dad called us in to eat.

28

I looked at the wall and noticed a big stripe where they forgot to paint. I leaned over to Blake and said, **"Now who's the one who needs help with self-monitoring?"**

29

"What do you mean?" Mom and Dad asked.
I pointed at the wall and said...

Seriously?
How did you
miss that?

They looked at each other,
and then at the same time said,
"Self-monitoring!"

And we all laughed.

Self-monitoring can be challenging to understand, and even more challenging to master. It covers a broad array of skills, such as completing work accurately and completely, staying on task, following instructions the first time, waiting to be called on, getting the teacher's attention appropriately, and others. While each of these skills should be taught and reinforced with children, the tips below provide some practical ways you can **help children develop their abilities to self-monitor.**

1. **Children always look to the adults** in their life as role models. Show children the strategies you use to monitor your work (lists, checking twice, slowing down, etc.).

2. **Create a checklist** of weekly chores or tasks a child has to do. Though the list is for the whole week, help break these chores/tasks up so they are spread across multiple days (based on the child's schedule) to help prepare him for success. At the end of the week, review with the child whether he accomplished all the tasks on the list. Praise him for successes, and make a plan for how to do better the following week if tasks were missed.

3. **Help children organize** their weekly homework so they can plan and prepare. Be sure to point out the days they are busy with extracurricular activities so they can adjust their homework schedule.

4. **If children are not taking** the proper materials home for homework or not finishing homework, make sure they are accurately recording assignments in their notebooks. Show them how to create visual prompts (a bright-colored reminder inside their desk or inside their homework folders).

5. **For teachers, having an established procedure for turning in homework** helps students be more successful. Consider putting a reminder prompt above the spot where students turn in homework that reminds them to double-check for common mistakes: *Is their name on the assignment? Did they answer every question? Are they putting the assignment in the correct folder or pile?*

6. **Don't be afraid to let your child fail.** Children learn from their mistakes. Just make sure you help your child reflect on her failures and come up with a new strategy to monitor her work.

7. **If your children need better ways to self-monitor,** make sure they understand why. Children are less likely to change their behavior if they do not believe there is a problem.

8. **Don't forget to praise!** Learning new skills or trying new things is hard. Be sure to praise your children when they practice self-monitoring, even when it's not perfect!

BOYS TOWN®
Saving Children Healing Families

Boys Town Press books by Bryan Smith
Kid-friendly books for teaching social skills

Executive **FUNction**

Downloadable Activities
Go to BoysTownPress.org
to download.

Of COURSE It's a **Big Deal!**
A Story about Learning to React Calmly and Appropriately
Written by Bryan Smith
Illustrated by Lisa M. Griffin

978-1-944882-11-2

TIME TO GET Started
A Story about Learning to Take Initiative
Illustrated by Lisa M. Griffin
Written by Bryan Smith

978-1-944882-31-0

It Was Just **Right Here!**
Written by Bryan Smith
Illustrated by Lisa M. Griffin

978-1-944882-20-4

What's the Problem?
A Story Teaching Problem Solving
Written by Bryan Smith
Illustrated by Lisa M. Griffin

978-1-944882-38-9

When I couldn't get Over it, I learned to **Start Acting Differently**
A story about managing SADness
Written by Bryan Smith
Illustrated by Lisa M. Griffin

978-1-944882-22-8

Is There an **APP for That?**
Written by Bryan Smith
Illustrated by Katie Wish
Hailey Discovers HAPPiness through Self-Acceptance

978-1-934490-74-7

OTHER TITLES: What Were You Thinking? and *My Day Is Ruined!*

DIVERSITY IS Key

WiTHOUT LiMiTS
dream · connect · soar

EMPATHY IS MY Superpower!
A Story about showing You care
Written by Bryan Smith
Illustrated by Lisa M. Griffin

MINDSET MATTERS
Written by Bryan Smith
Illustrated by Lisa Griffin

Kindness Counts
a story for teaching random acts of kindness
Written by Bryan Smith
Illustrated by Brian Martin

STRESS STINKS
Written by Bryan Smith
Illustrated by Lisa M. Griffin

The National Parenting Center Seal of Approval
IF WINNING ISN'T **EVERYTHING, WHY DO I HATE TO LOSE?**
Written by BRYAN SMITH
Illustrated by BRIAN MARTIN

978-1-934490-85-3

978-1-944882-36-5

978-1-944882-29-7

978-1-944882-12-9

978-1-944882-01-3

978-1-944882-46-4

BOYS TOWN® Press

For information on Boys Town and its Education Model, Common Sense Parenting®, and training programs:
boystowntraining.org | boystown.org/parenting
training@BoysTown.org | 1-800-545-5771

For parenting and educational books and other resources:
BoysTownPress.org
btpress@BoysTown.org | 1-800-282-6657